Bill's New Frock

Illustrated by Philippe Dupasquier

His mother swept out, leaving him staring in
dismay at the mirror. In it, a girl with his curly
red hair and wearing a pretty pink frock with
fiddly shell buttons was staring back at him in
equal dismay.

'This can't be true', Bill Simpson said to himself. 'This cannot be true!'

Also by Anne Fine

The Book of the Banshee
Flour Babies
Goggle-Eyes
The Granny Project
Madame Doubtfire
The Other Darker Ned
A Pack of Liars
Round behind the Icehouse
The Stone Menagerie
The Summer House Loon

for younger readers

The Angel of Nitshill Road
Anneli the Art Hater
The Chicken Gave it to Me
The Country Pancake
Crummy Mummy and Me
Design a Pram
Only a Show
Scaredy Cat
Stranger Danger
A Sudden Puff of Glittering Smoke
A Sudden Swirl of Icy Wind
A Sudden Glow of Gold

ANNE FINE

Bill's New Frock

MAMMOTH

First published in Great Britain 1989
by Methuen Children's Books
Published 1990 by Mammoth Books
an imprint of Reed Consumer Books Limited
Michelin House, 81 Fulham Road, London SW3 6RB
and Auckland, Melbourne, Singapore and Toronto

Reprinted 1990 (five times), 1991 (five times), 1992 (three times),
1993 (four times)

Text copyright © 1989 Anne Fine
Illustrations copyright © 1989 Philippe Dupasquier

ISBN 0 7497 0305 9

A CIP catalogue record for this title
is available from the British Library

Printed and bound in Great Britain by
BPCC Paperbacks Ltd
Member of BPCC Ltd

Contents

· 1 ·

A Really Awful Start

When Bill Simpson woke up on Monday morning, he found he was a girl.

He was still standing staring at himself in the mirror, quite baffled, when his mother swept in.

'Why don't you wear this pretty pink dress?' she said.

'I *never* wear dresses,' Bill burst out.

'I know,' his mother said. 'It's such a pity.'

And, to his astonishment, before he could even begin to argue, she had dropped the dress over his head and zipped up the back.

'I'll leave you to do up the shell buttons,' she said. 'They're a bit fiddly and I'm late for work.'

And she swept out, leaving him staring in dismay at the mirror. In it, a girl with his curly red hair and wearing a pretty pink frock with fiddly shell buttons was staring back at him in equal dismay.

'This can't be true,' Bill Simpson said to himself. 'This cannot be true!'

He stepped out of his bedroom just as his father was rushing past. He, too, was late in getting off to work.

Mr Simpson leaned over and planted a kiss on Bill's cheek.

'Bye, Poppet,' he said, ruffling Bill's curls. 'You look very sweet today. It's not often we see you in a frock, is it?'

He ran down the stairs and out of the

house so quickly he didn't see Bill's scowl, or hear what he muttered savagely under his breath.

Bella the cat didn't seem to notice any difference. She purred and rubbed her soft, furry body around his ankles in exactly the same way as she always did.

And Bill found himself spooning up his cornflakes as usual. It was as if he couldn't help it. He left the house at the usual time, too. He didn't seem to have any choice. Things, though odd, were just going on in their own way, as in a dream.

Or it could be a nightmare! For hanging about on the corner was the gang of boys from the other school. Bill recognised the one they called Mean Malcolm in his purple studded jacket.

I think I'll go round the long way instead, Bill thought to himself. I don't want to be tripped up in one of their nasty scuffles, like last week, when all the scabs were kicked off my ankle.

Then Bill heard the most piercing whistle.

He looked around to see where the noise was coming from, then realised Mean Malcolm was whistling at him!

Bill Simpson blushed so pink that all his freckles disappeared. He felt so foolish he forgot to turn off at the next corner to go round the long way. He ended up walking right past the gang.

Mean Malcolm just sprawled against the railings, whistling at Bill as he went by wearing his pretty pink frock with shell buttons.

Bill Simpson thought to himself: I'd rather have the scabs kicked off my ankle!

When he reached the main road, there was an elderly woman with curly grey hair already standing at the kerb. To feel safe from the gang, he stood at her side.

'Give me your hand, little girl,' she said. 'I'll see us both safely across the road.'

'No, really,' insisted Bill. 'I'm fine, honestly. I cross here every day by myself.'

The woman simply didn't listen. She just

11

reached down and grasped his wrist, hauling him after her across the road.

On the far side, she looked down approvingly as she released him.

'That's such a pretty frock!' she said. 'You mind you keep it nice and clean.'

Rather than say something disagreeable, Bill ran off quickly.

The headmaster was standing at the school gates, holding his watch in the palm of his hand, watching the last few stragglers arrive.

'Get your skates on, Stephen Irwin!' he yelled. And: '*Move*, Tom Warren!'

Another boy charged round the corner and cut in front of Bill.

'Late, Andrew!' the headmaster called out fiercely. 'Late, late, late!'

Then it was Bill's turn to go past.

'That's right,' the headmaster called out encouragingly. 'Hurry along, dear. We don't want to miss assembly, do we?'

And he followed Bill up the path to the school.

Assembly always took place in the main hall. After the hymn, everyone was told to sit on the floor, as usual. Desperately, Bill tried to tuck the pretty pink dress in tightly around his bare legs.

Mrs Collins leaned forward on her canvas chair.

'Stop fidgeting with your frock, dear,' she told him. 'You're getting nasty, grubby fingerprints all round the hem.'

Bill glowered all through the rest of assembly. At the end, everybody stood up as usual.

'Now I need four strong volunteers to carry a table across to the nursery,' announced the headmaster. 'Who wants to go?'

Practically everybody in the hall raised a hand. Everyone liked a trip over the playground. In the nursery they had music and water and bright sloshy paints and tricycles and enormous lego. And if you kept your head down and didn't talk too much or too loudly, it might be a good few minutes before anyone realised you were really from

13

one of the other classrooms, and shooed you back.

So the hall was a mass of waving hands.

The headmaster gazed around him.

Then he picked four boys.

On the way out of the hall, Bill Simpson heard Astrid complaining to Mrs Collins:

'It isn't fair! He *always* picks the boys to carry things.'

'Perhaps the table's quite heavy,' soothed Mrs Collins.

'None of the tables in this school are heavy,' said Astrid. 'And I know for a fact that I am stronger than at least two of the boys he picked.'

'It's true,' Bill said. 'Whenever we have a tug of war, everyone wants to have Astrid on their team.'

'Oh, well,' said Mrs Collins. 'It doesn't matter. No need to make such a fuss over nothing. It's only a silly old table.'

And when Astrid and Bill took up arguing again, she told them the subject was closed, rather sharply.

Back in the classroom, everyone settled down at their tables.

'We'll do our writing first, shall we?' said Mrs Collins. 'And after that, we'll reward ourselves with a story.'

While Mrs Collins handed out the writing books and everyone scrabbled for pencils and rubbers, Bill looked round his table.

He was the only one in a dress.

Flora was wearing trousers and a blue blouse. Kirsty and Nick were both wearing jeans and a shirt. Philip was wearing corduroy slacks and a red jumper, and Talilah wore bright red satin bloomers under her fancy silk top.

Yes, there was no doubt about it. Talilah looked snazzy enough to go dancing, but Bill was the only one in a frock.

Oh, this was awful! What on earth had happened? Why didn't anybody seem to have noticed? What could he do? When would it end?

Bill Simpson put his head in his hands, and covered his eyes.

15

'On with your work down there on table five,' warned Mrs Collins promptly.

She meant him. He knew it. So Bill picked up his pen and opened his books. He couldn't help it. He didn't seem to have any choice. Things were still going on in their own way, as in a dream.

He wrote more than he usually did. He wrote it more neatly than usual, too. If you looked back through the last few pages of his work, you'd see he'd done a really good job, for him.

But you wouldn't have thought so, the way Mrs Collins went on when she saw it.

'Look at this,' she scolded, stabbing her finger down on the page. 'This isn't very neat, is it? Look at this dirty smudge. And the edge of your book looks as if it's been *chewed!*'

She turned to Philip to inspect his book next. It was far messier than Bill's. It was more smudgy and more chewed-looking. The writing was untidy and irregular. Some of the letters were so enormous they looked

like giants herding the smaller letters haphazardly across the page.

'Not bad at all, Philip,' she said. 'Keep up the good work.'

Bill could scarcely believe his ears. He was outraged. As soon as she'd moved off, he reached out for Philip's book, laid it beside his own on the table, and compared the two.

'It isn't fair!' he complained bitterly. 'Your page is *much* worse than my page. She didn't say anything nice to *me*.'

Philip just shrugged and said:

'Well, girls are neater.'

Bill felt so cross he had to sit on his hands to stop himself from thumping Philip.

Up at her desk, Mrs Collins was leafing through the class reader: *Tales of Today and Yesterday*.

'Where are we?' she asked them. 'Where did we finish last week? Did we get to the end of *Polly the Pilot*?'

She turned the page.

'Ah!' she said. 'Here's a good old story you all know perfectly well, I'm sure. It's

Rapunzel. And today it's table five's turn to take the main parts.'

Looking up, she eyed all six of them sitting there waiting.

'You'll be the farmer,' she said to Nick. 'You be the farmer's wife,' to Talilah. 'Witch,' she said to Flora. 'Prince,' she said to Philip. 'Narrator,' she said to Kirsty.

Oh, no! Oh, no! Bill held his breath as Mrs Collins looked at him and said:

'The Lovely Rapunzel.'

Before Bill could protest, Talilah had started reading aloud. She and the farmer began with a furious argument about whether or not it was safe to steal a lettuce from the garden of the wicked witch next door, to feed their precious daughter Rapunzel. Once they'd got going, Bill didn't like to interrupt them, so he just sat and flicked over the pages, looking for his first speech.

It was a long wait. The Lovely Rapunzel didn't seem to *do* very much. She just got stolen out of spite by the Witch, and hidden

19

away at the very top of a high stone tower which had no door. There she just sat quietly for about fifteen years, being no trouble and growing her hair.

She didn't try to escape. She didn't complain. She didn't even have any fights with the Witch.

So far as Bill Simpson could make out, she wasn't really worth rescuing. He wasn't at all sure why the Prince bothered. He certainly wouldn't have made the effort himself.

After three pages, there came a bit for Rapunzel.

'Oooooooooh!' Bill read out aloud. 'Ooooooooooh!'

No, it wasn't much of a part. Or much of a life, come to that, if you thought about it.

Bill raised his hand. He couldn't help it.

'Yes?' Mrs Collins said. 'What's the problem?' She hated interruptions when they were reading.

'I don't see why Rapunzel just has to sit and wait for the Prince to come along and rescue her,' explained Bill. 'Why couldn't she plan her own escape? Why didn't she cut off all her lovely long hair herself, and braid it into a rope, and knot the rope to something, and then slide down it? Why did she have to just sit there and waste fifteen years waiting for a Prince?'

Mrs Collins narrowed her eyes at Bill Simpson.

'You're in a very funny mood today,' she

told him. 'Are you sure that you're feeling quite yourself?'

Was he feeling quite himself? In this frock? Bill stared around the room. Everyone's eyes were on him. They were all waiting to hear what he said. What could he say?

Mercifully, before he was forced to answer, the bell rang for playtime.

· 2 ·

The Wumpy Choo

Outside in the playground a few boys were
already kicking a football about. Bill Simpson
was just about to charge in and join them
when he remembered what he was wearing.
He'd look a bit daft if he took a tumble, he
decided. Maybe just for once he'd try to think
of something else to do during playtime.

23

Each boy who ran out of the school joined the football game on one side or another. What did the girls do? He looked around. Some perched along the nursery wall, chatting to one another. Others stood in the cloakroom porch, -sharing secrets and giggling. There were a few more huddled in each corner of the playground. Each time the football came their way, one of them would give it a hefty boot back into the game. There were two girls trying to mark out a hopscotch frame; but every time the footballers ran over the lines they were drawing, the chalk was so badly scuffed that you couldn't see the squares any longer.

But it was rather chilly just standing about. The dress might be very pretty, but it was thin, and Bill's legs were bare. He decided to join the girls in the porch. At least they were out of the wind.

As he came up to them, Leila was saying: 'Martin bets no one dares kick a football straight through the cloakroom window!'

The girls all looked up at the cloakroom

window. So did Bill. As usual, the caretaker had pushed up the lower half of the window as far as it would go. It made quite a large square hole.

'*Anyone* could kick a football through there,' scoffed Kirsty.

'*I* could,' said Astrid.

'Easy,' agreed Leila.

'What do you get if you do it?' Bill asked them.

'A wumpy choo.'

'A wumpy choo?'

Bill Simpson was mystified.

'Yes,' Leila told him. 'A wumpy choo.'

Bill glanced round the little group of girls. Nobody else looked in the least bit baffled. Presumably they all knew about wumpy choos – whatever they were.

'I didn't know you could get wumpy choos round here,' said Flora.

So they were rare, were they? Like giant pandas.

'I'd *love* a wumpy choo,' said Sarah. 'But I'm not allowed because I'm allergic.'

26

Definitely an animal, then. A furry one. Bill's next door neighbour was allergic to furry animals, too.

'What colour is it?' asked Astrid. 'Is it a pink one?'

If it was still pink, thought Bill, it was probably a baby and hadn't grown a lot of fur.

'No,' Linda told them. 'I know exactly what colour it is because it's the very last one, and it's browny-yellow.'

Perhaps Martin hadn't been feeding it properly. Perhaps that was the reason its nice pink skin and fur had gone all browny-yellow.

Obviously it needed to be rescued – and fast!

He'd better take the bet.

'I'll do it,' he announced. 'I'll kick the football through the cloakroom window, and get the wumpy choo.'

Talilah gave him a bit of a look.

'You'd better be careful of your dress,' she warned. 'That football is filthy.'

27

'I'll manage,' said Bill Simpson. 'I know what I'm doing.'

The news, he noticed, spread like wildfire all along the line of girls perched on the nursery wall, and into the little huddles in the corners of the playground. All the girls turned to watch someone have a go at kicking a football straight through the cloakroom window.

'What's the bet?' they asked one another.

'A wumpy choo.'

Right then, thought Bill. No reason to hang about. It was a simple enough shot. All he needed was a football.

He walked towards the footballers in order to borrow theirs for a moment. Just as he did so, the game happened to swing his way and several boys charged past – knocking Bill flat on his back on the tarmac.

'Get out of the way!'

'*We're* playing here!'

Bill picked himself up. He was astonished. Usually if anyone walked into the football game, the players just thought they'd decided to join in. 'Come in on *our* side!' they'd yell. 'Be our goalie! Take over!'

This time it was as if they weren't so much playing football around him as *through* him.

'Get off the pitch!'

'Stop getting in our way! Go *round*!'

It was the frock again! He knew it!

'I want the ball,' yelled Bill to all the other players. 'I just want to borrow it for a minute – for a bet!'

Games always stopped for bets. It was a rule. But they all acted as if they hadn't even heard him.

'Out of our *way*!'

'You're spoiling the *game*!'

The ball happened to bounce Bill's way again, so he leaped up and caught it in his hands.

'I *need* it,' he explained. 'Just for a moment.'

The footballers gathered in a circle round him. They didn't look at all pleased at this interruption of the game. In fact, they

looked rather menacing, all standing there with narrowed eyes, scowling. If this was the sort of reception the girls had come to expect, no wonder they didn't stray far from the railings. No wonder they didn't ask to play.

'Give the ball back,' Rohan was really glowering now.

'Yes,' Martin agreed. 'Why can't you stay in your own bit of the playground?'

Mystified, Bill asked Martin:

'What bit?'

'The girls' bit, of course.'

Bill looked around. Girls were still perched along the nursery wall. Girls were still huddled in the porch. Girls still stood in tight little groups in each corner. No girl was more than a few feet into the playground itself. Even the pair who had been trying to mark out the hopscotch game had given up and gone away.

'Where's that, then?' asked Bill. 'Where's the girls' bit? Where *are* the girls supposed to play?'

'*I* don't know,' Martin answered irritably. '*Anywhere*. Just somewhere we're not already playing football.'

'But you're playing football all over *every single inch* of the playground!'

Martin glanced up at the clock on the church tower next door to the school. There were only two minutes left before the bell rang, and his team was down by one tiny goal.

He spread his hands in desperation.

'*Please* give the ball back,' he pleaded. 'What's it worth?'

For the life of him Bill Simpson couldn't understand why, if Martin wanted the ball back so badly, he couldn't just step forward and try to prise it away from his chest. Then he realised that Martin simply didn't dare. The two of them might end up in a bit of a shoving match, and then a real fight – and *no one* fights a girl in a pretty pink frock with fiddly shell buttons.

So he said cunningly:

'I'll tell you what it's worth. It's worth your very last wumpy choo!'

To his astonishment, Martin looked delighted.

'Done!' he said at once, and began digging deep in his trouser pocket.

He handed a tiny, wrappered rectangle over to Bill.

'There you are,' he said. 'Here it is. Now give me the football and get off the pitch!'

Bill Simpson looked down.

'What's this?' he asked.

'It's what you wanted,' Martin said. 'My very last 1p Chew.'

In silence, Bill Simpson handed over the football. Where he'd been clutching it tightly against his chest, there was now an enormous brown smudge.

In silence, Bill Simpson turned and walked away. If all the girls had not been standing around the edges of the playground watching him, he would have cried.

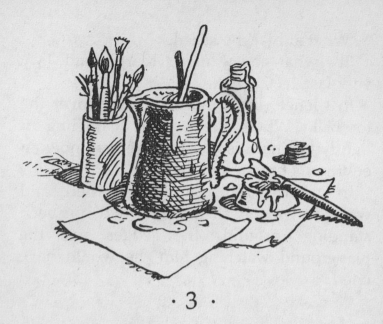

· 3 ·

Pink, Pink,
Nothing But Pink

After break, it was art. Everyone helped to unfold the large, crackling plastic sheets and lay them over the table tops, and spread old newspapers over them. Then Mrs Collins sent Leila into the dark cupboard at the back of the classroom to see what was left in the art supplies box.

'Are there any coloured chalks left?'

'No, they're all gone.'

'Pastels, then.'

'They're still too damp to use after the roof leak.'

'What about clay?'

'It's all dried up.'

'There *must* be crayons. *Every* class has crayons.'

'The infants came and borrowed ours last week, and haven't brought them back yet.'

'Right, then. It will just have to be paint, as usual.'

So Leila dragged the heavy cardboard box full of paint tubs out of the cupboard, and everyone crowded round to choose their colours.

'Here's a pink.'

'What's that?'

'Pink.'

'More pink.'

'Pink.'

'I've found some blue – no, I haven't. It's empty.'

'I thought I'd found some green, but it's dried up.'

'There's no white. There's never any white. We haven't had white for years and years.'

'There's some pink here.'

'And this one's pink.'

'Pink, pink, nothing but pink!'

Everyone stood up, disappointed. Kirsty voiced everyone's disgust:

'What can you do with pink?' she demanded. 'You can't paint pink dogs or pink space vehicles or pink trees or pink battlefields, can you? If you can only find one colour, it's difficult enough. But if you've only got pink, it's practically *impossible*. What is there in the world that's all pink?'

'Yes. What's all pink?'

Everyone gazed around the room, looking for something that was all pink so they could paint it. Some of them stared at the pictures and posters pinned on the classroom walls. Others gazed out of the window, across the playground to the street and the shops. One or two of them glanced at one another –

And Kirsty looked at Bill.

'No!' Bill said. 'No, no, no! Not me! Absolutely not! You can't!'

Now everyone turned to look at Bill.

'No!' Bill insisted. 'I am *not all pink*!'

Now even Mrs Collins was looking at Bill.

'Pink frock,' she admitted slowly. 'And fiery hair. Rich rosy freckles and a nice deep blush. Yes, you'll do beautifully, dear. You're all pink.'

'I am *not pink*.'

But he was getting pinker by the minute. And by the time everyone had wandered back to their seats clutching their little plastic tubs of paint, you wouldn't have needed any other colour to do a really fine portrait of him.

'Perfect!' said Mrs Collins.

And taking Bill Simpson firmly by the hand, she tried to lead him over towards a chair in the middle of the room, where everyone would be able to see him clearly while they were painting him.

Bill tried to pull back. Mrs Collins turned in astonishment at his unwillingness, and let go of his hand quite suddenly. Bill staggered back – straight into Nicky who had just prised the top off his paint tub.

A huge glob of pink paint flew up in the air, and landed on Bill Simpson's frock. As everyone watched, it gathered itself, all fat and heavy at the bottom. Then, slowly, it slithered down between the folds of material, leaving a thick pink slug trail.

Bill Simpson watched in silence as a small pool of pink paint appeared on the floor, beside his left foot.

Grubby fingerprints round the hem; a huge muddy smudge on the front; a great slimy paint smear down the side. What next?

Mrs Collins inspected the damage, and shrugged.

'Well, never mind,' she said. 'It's only poster paint. I'm sure the frock will wash out beautifully.'

And, once again, she took his hand.

There was no fight left in Bill Simpson. Meekly, he allowed himself to be led to the middle of the room.

Mrs Collins arranged him neatly and comfortably on the little wooden chair.

'There,' she said triumphantly, placing a cherry-coloured exercise book in one of his hands as a last touch. 'All pink!'

She stepped back to admire her handiwork.

'Perfect!' she said again. 'Now is everyone happy?'

Bill Simpson could have tried to say something then, but he didn't bother. He reckoned there was no point. He knew that, whatever he said and whatever he did, this awful day would just keep sailing on in its own way, as in a dream. A curse was on him. A pink curse. He was, of all things, haunted by a pretty pink frock with fiddly shell buttons. He might as well give up struggling. Like poor Rapunzel trapped in her high stone tower, he'd just sit quietly, waiting to see what happened, hoping for rescue.

Meanwhile, the rest of the class had begun to complain.

'If we've only got pink to paint with, how are we supposed to do that great big

football-shaped smudge on the front of the frock? It's *brown*!'

'I can't paint all those grubby little fingerprints right round the hem of the dress, because they're *grey*.'

'Those shell buttons are a bit fiddly to paint!'

'I've done far too many freckles. What shall I do?'

'Wait till they're dry, then chip some off!'

Bill ignored everyone. He just sat there, waiting for time to go by. Even a bad dream couldn't last forever. His torment had to end some time, surely.

After half an hour or so, Mrs Collins came by, carrying a fresh jar of water over to table two.

'Do try not to look quite so *gloomy*, dear,' she murmured in Bill's ear as she walked past. 'You're spoiling people's paintings.'

And Bill was too miserable and defeated even to bother to scowl at the back of her head as she moved off.

· 4 ·

No Pockets

Perhaps Mrs Collins noticed how fed up he looked. Perhaps she was grateful to him for sitting so still for so long, and being so pink. Or maybe it was just Bill's eye she happened to catch first. But, whatever the reason, it was Bill Simpson she chose to take her spare key back to the office.

'That's helpful of you,' she said, pressing the key into his hand. 'Just give it to Mrs Bandaraina. She's expecting it. And hurry back.'

Everyone else looked up from their maths books and watched enviously as he left the classroom and shut the door firmly behind him.

Outside, in the deserted corridor, one thought and one thought only was in Bill Simpson's mind: lavatories! Silently he crept along. Should he turn left, into the BOYS, and risk hoots and catcalls of astonishment if anyone caught him there in his pretty pink frock? Or should he turn right, into the GIRLS, where for a boy even to be found hanging around the doorway was to risk terrible trouble?

Girls' lavatories were more *private*. At least he could struggle with the frock in peace . . .

Bill made his choice. Peering back over his shoulder like some spy from an old black and white film, he scuttled hastily into the GIRLS.

When, two minutes later, he stuck his head back out through the swing doors, the

45

corridor was still empty. Sighing with relief, Bill stepped out. He took his time now, dawdling along towards the school office, swinging the key from his fingers and stopping to peer at each painting on the wall. After his heart-stopping rush in and out of the

girls' lavatories, Bill reckoned that he'd earned a break.

But just as he turned the corner, who should he see backing out of a cupboard but the headmaster!

Bill Simpson started looking sharp. Lifting his chin, he walked a lot faster. He was almost safely past the headmaster when he was stopped.

A hand fell on the top of his head.

'You look very sensible and responsible,' the headmaster said. 'Not dawdling along, peering at all the paintings, taking your time. Are you going to the office on an errand for your teacher? Would you do me a favour and take these coloured inks to Mrs Bandaraina?'

And he held out a handful of tiny glass bottles.

Bill put out his free hand, and the headmaster tipped the tiny glass bottles onto his outstretched palm.

'Whatever you do, don't drop them,' he warned. And then he dived back in his cupboard.

Bill went on. He'd hardly reached the short flight of stairs when the school nurse came up them the other way, carrying a pile of yellow forms in her arms, and walking faster than most people run.

'Ah!' she said, spotting Bill. 'Just what I need! Someone who can take these medical forms to the office for me, so I can rush straight across to the nursery before the bell rings.'

She didn't exactly ask. And she didn't exactly wait to see if Bill minded. She just thrust the stack of yellow medical forms into his arms, and hurried off.

'And they're in perfect, alphabetical order,' she called back over her shoulder. 'So, whatever you do, don't drop them!'

Problem, thought Bill. One false move, and everything would fall to the floor – spare key, little glass ink bottles, medical forms in perfect, alphabetical order – the lot.

The key and the coloured inks would just have to go in his pockets.

Pockets?

Carefully, Bill squatted in the corridor and

48

lowered the pile of yellow medical forms to the floor, taking care that he didn't lose the key or drop the little glass bottles of coloured ink.

Then he felt all round the pretty pink frock for a pocket. He pushed and shoved at rather frilly places here and there, wherever he thought one might be hidden. But though he heard the material rip once or twice, and felt his hands go through the holes he'd accidentally torn, there were no pockets there.

No. Not one pocket. Yards and yards of material. Pleats, frills, bows, scallops, fancy loops. But not one pocket. Whoever designed the dress had gone to all the trouble of matching the imitation lace round the hem with the imitation lace round the collar, and fitting a zip in so neatly that it was practically invisible, and putting comfortable elastic around the little puffy sleeves.

But they just hadn't bothered to put in a pocket.

Bill was *amazed*. How was a person in a frock like this supposed to *survive*? How were they expected to get along without any

49

pockets? It can't have been the only dress of its kind that was made. Other people must wear them. Where did they put their money, for heaven's sake? Did they keep it, all damp and hot and sticky, in the palms of their hands all day? Where did they put the sweets their friends gave them if they wanted to save them for later? What did they do if someone returned their pencil sharpener to them outside in break?

How can you *live* without pockets? How can you? How *can* you?

Bill put his head in his hands, and groaned.

Then he tried to pull himself together. This couldn't last forever. This couldn't go on. No boy could turn into a girl and stay that way without anyone – even his mother and teacher and schoolfriends – noticing any real difference. It must be a bad dream. It *felt* like a nightmare . . .

He'd just keep calm and steady and wait till the horror of it all was over. He'd just get on with the job in hand.

And the job in hand was to get all these things safely to the school office.

Bill gathered up the yellow medical forms. On top of them he put the coloured inks, right in the middle so they would not roll over the edge and smash on the floor. He wedged the key between the inks so it would not slide off the side. Then, very carefully, he started down the corridor again, towards the office.

Before he'd gone a dozen steps, he heard a rapping on the nearest window.

He turned to look. It was the caretaker.

The caretaker leaned through the window.

'Off to the office, are you?' he asked. 'Do us a favour. Take these tennis balls with you. Ask Mrs Bandaraina to lock them away.'

And before Bill could argue, the caretaker tipped seven tennis balls onto the carefully stacked pile in Bill's arms.

Bill stood for a moment, steadying his load. He let the medical forms dip a bit in the middle to make a sort of hollow to keep the balls together and stop them rolling off over every side. Then, even more carefully than before – step by tiny, gentle step – he made for the office again.

When he was only a few yards away he saw Mrs Bandaraina lift her head from her typing and glance through the open doorway and notice him, shuffling, barely an inch at a time, towards her.

Each step seemed to take forever. Everything in his pile seemed to be wobbling dangerously. Everything in his pile seemed to be sliding closer to the edge.

'My!' Mrs Bandaraina said, watching his snail-slow progress. 'Aren't you the careful one, taking such care not to spill coloured ink on your sweet little frock!'

It wasn't Bill's fault. It was because she said 'sweet little frock!'. A shudder of pure fury rose through his body and made his hands shake. He didn't know the yellow forms were going to slip from his grasp and slither out of alphabetical order across the floor. He didn't know the little glass bottles would fall and smash. He didn't know the seven tennis balls would bounce up and down in the bright coloured pools of spilt inks. He didn't know the spare key would end up submerged in a puddle of purple.

Bill Simpson tried very hard not to narrow his eyes at Mrs Bandaraina and blame her for everything as she slid off her office chair to help him. He tried very hard to look grateful as she swept a handful of tissues out of the box on her desk and helped him mop and wipe, and gather rainbow- spotted tennis balls. And he tried to look pleasant while she tipped the slivers of shattered glass in the waste basket, and helped him shuffle all the medical forms back into alphabetical order.

But once back in the corridor again, and alone, he couldn't help muttering something quite rude, and quite loudly, about the sort of person who would design a pretty pink frock with no pockets, and expect other people to go around wearing it.

· 5 ·

The Big Fight

It rained all through the lunch hour. The sky went grey, the windows misted over, and from overhead came the steady gunfire sound of huge raindrops pinging smartly on the skylight.

And Mrs Collins slipped into one of her dark wet-break moods.

Everyone knew the signs: the eyebrows knitting together over her nose; the lines across her forehead deepening to furrows; her lips thinning into tightened purse strings.

Everyone knew it was not the time to cause trouble.

So as the rain beat heavily against the window panes, everyone crept quietly around the classroom, trying to look as if they were up to something useful or sensible, or, at the very least, quiet.

And out of the storeroom came the old comic box.

Nobody *meant* to make a great noise and a fuss. All anyone wanted was simply to go to the box, dip in their hand, and pick out a couple of comics they liked. Nobody *meant* to end up in a scrum, pushing and shoving the others out of the way, using their elbows, desperate to get an arm in and whip out a favourite comic before someone else leaned over and snatched it.

Nobody *meant* to end up in a riot.

'SILENCE!' roared Mrs Collins. 'Go back to

your places at once! I will give out the comics *myself.'*

As she came over, everyone melted away from the comic box and drifted back to their own favourite wet-break places. Talilah and Kirsty sat side by side on the fat radiator pipes. Flora perched on the window sill. Philip and Nicky sprawled on the floor beneath table five, and Bill, who probably would have joined them on any other wet day, glanced down at all the marks and smears and tears he already had on his pretty pink frock, and then at the muddy grime and footprints all over the floor where his friends were – and thought better of it.

He settled himself alone, leaning his chair back against the wall, and waited for Mrs Collins to hand round the comics.

They were a shabby and a dog-eared lot. It was with a slight shudder of disgust that Mrs Collins dipped her arms in the box to lift them out, and started round the room. Like everyone else, Bill hoped so hard that she would go round his way first, but he was out of luck.

She went the other way. It took her ages.

All of the Beanos went first, of course. Then all the Dandies. She gave out a Hotspur and a Lion, then several Bunties and some Victors.

By the time she reached Bill Simpson, there was very little left.

'Mandy?' she offered him. 'Or would you prefer a June or a Judy?'

He could tell from the look on her face that she wasn't in the mood for discussion. So he contented himself with replying coldly:

'I'll have a Thunder, please. Or a Hornet.'

'No more Hornets,' she said, leafing through the last three or four comics left in her hand. 'No Thunders, either. I thought I might still have a Valiant, but I must have given that to Rohan.'

She thrust a Bunty towards him.

'There you are,' she said. 'You'll enjoy this. There's almost no pages missing at all.'

And off she went, back to her desk.

Bill glanced down at the comic in his hands. He didn't care for the look of it at all. He didn't want to read it. What use was a Bunty?

He wanted a Beano or a Dandy or a Thunder, and that was that.

Melissa was sitting only a few feet away, absorbed in a Beano.

Bill leaned across.

'Hey, Melissa,' he called softly. 'Here's a Bunty with all the pages and no torn bits. Do you want to swap?'

Melissa gazed at him over her comic, her eyes widening even more as she realized he was serious.

'You must be *joking*,' she said, and went back to her Beano.

Bill tried the other side.

Flora was sitting firmly on one Dandy, and reading another.

'Flora,' called Bill. 'Would you like a Bunty?'

'No, thank you,' Flora said politely, without so much as raising her eyes from the page.

Bill Simpson decided to have a go at one of the boys.

'Rohan!' he hissed. 'Hey! Rohan! I'll swap you my practically brand new comic here for

59

your tatty old Valiant with hardly any pages left.'

'What's your comic?' asked Rohan. 'Is it a Hotspur?'

'No,' Bill confessed. 'No. It's a Bunty.'

Rohan just sniggered and went back to his comic. Clearly he thought it was just a good joke.

Bill tried one last time.

'Martin,' he offered. 'Will you swap with me as soon as you've finished that Victor?'

Martin said:

'Sure. What have you got there?'

Bill said as softly as he could:

'Bunty.'

'What?' Martin said. *'What?'*

So Bill Simpson had to tell him all over again.

Martin snorted.

'No thanks,' he said. 'No *thanks*. I'll swap mine with Melissa's Beano instead.'

And he went back to his reading.

Bill blamed Mrs Collins, frankly. Though he couldn't prove it, and wouldn't dare ask, he firmly suspected that, if he had not been wearing the pretty pink frock, he would never have ended up with the Bunty. Mrs Collins could easily have arranged things some other way. She might have ordered Flora to give

61

him the Dandy she was sitting on, to keep him going. Or she might have suggested to Rohan that Bill and he sit close together to read the Valiant at the same time.

He couldn't prove it – no, he couldn't prove it. But he felt sore about it all the same.

But clearly there was nothing to be done now. It was too late. Everyone else was reading quietly, and Mrs Collins didn't look as if she would take at all kindly to any complaints. He could either waste the whole lunch break trying, completely in vain, to find someone who would trade their comic for his Bunty, or he could give up and just read the Bunty.

He read the Bunty.

And it wasn't that bad. He read the story about the sneaky schoolteacher who switched the examination papers around so that her own spoilt and lazy daughter would win the one and only college place. He read the story about the brave orphan gypsy girl who led her lame pony carefully at night through a dangerous war zone. He was still quite absorbed in the very funny tale of three girls who had somehow found themselves responsible for an enormous hippopotamus with an even more enormous appetite, when a shadow fell over the page.

Flora was holding out a Dandy.

'Swap?'

'In a minute. Let me finish this.'

'Now or never,' said Flora.

'All right, then,' said Bill.

A little regretfully – he wouldn't have minded finding out what the hippo ate next – Bill handed over his Bunty and took the Dandy. No sooner had he turned the first page than yet another shadow fell on him, and Rohan was standing at his side.

'Here. You take this, and I'll have that one.'

In his hand, Rohan held a copy of June.

'No, thanks,' said Bill, and he went back to his reading.

'Come on,' said Rohan. 'Don't be mean. Swap comics with me. I don't want this one.'

'I don't want it either.'

'You haven't read it.'

'I am reading *this*.'

And Bill shook his Dandy in Rohan's face.

That was his first big mistake. His second big mistake was not moving fast enough when Rohan reached out and tried to snatch it.

Rohan's grip tightened over the top of the comic.

'Let go of my Dandy!'

'Don't be so *mean*!'

'*Mean*? Why *should* I give you my Dandy and take your rotten June?'

'Because you might *like* it,' said Rohan. 'And I definitely *won't*.'

The penny dropped. It was the frock again. Bill couldn't believe it. Hadn't the morning been agonising enough? Now was even his lunch break going to be ruined because he just happened to be wearing this stupid, silly curse of a dress? If this was the sort of thing that kept happening to you if you came to school in a frilly pink frock, no wonder all the girls wore jeans!

Bill Simpson had had quite enough.

'Let go of my comic,' he warned Rohan in a soft and dangerous voice. 'Let go of it or I shall mash you.'

In answer to this threat, Rohan tugged harder.

The Dandy began to tear.

'Let go!' repeated Bill Simpson.

Rohan pulled harder. Bill Simpson hit him. He clenched his fist and punched Rohan on the shoulder as hard as he could.

Rohan yelped in pain, and dropped his half of the comic.

Though his heart was thumping so fiercely

his eyes couldn't settle on the pictures, let alone read the print, Bill Simpson pretended he had calmly gone back to his Dandy.

Until Rohan kicked out at him.

In fact, his foot didn't touch Bill at all. It tangled instead in the folds of the pretty pink dress. But it did leave a great, black criss-cross footprint on the flimsy material, and it was a kick.

And Bill was furious. He leaped to his feet and started hitting Rohan as hard as he could. Rohan put up his own fists to defend himself. And, within seconds, they were having a fight.

The noise was tremendous. Everyone in the classroom started up at once – some asking who had started the fight, some egging on one side or another, some telling both of them to stop.

Then, as the blows rained down on either side, everyone around fell silent. For this was the first really big fight ever seen in the classroom itself, and it was shocking. No one was ever surprised to see the odd, sly kick on someone's ankle. Everyone had noticed the occasional deliberate tripping up, or hard nudge.

But nothing like this. Not a real big fight. Never.

It was Mrs Collins who put a stop to it. Striding across the room in a fury, she grasped both of them by the shoulder and hauled them apart.

Both were scarlet with rage.

'How *dare* you?' shouted Mrs Collins. 'How DARE you?'

She was enraged, too. No one had ever seen her looking so angry. Her dark wet-break mood had turned so fierce she looked fit to kill. Her eyes were flashing, her nose gone pointy, and her mouth shrunk to a lemon-sucking sliver.

'How *dare* you!'

Rohan and Bill stood glowering at one another.

'What *is* going on? Who *started* this fight?'

'It wasn't *my* fault,' snarled Rohan. '*I* didn't start it.'

'You *did*,' snarled Bill, clenching his fists again. 'You *kicked* me!'

He showed the footprint on his pretty pink frock.

'You punched me first,' insisted Rohan, rubbing his shoulder hard to try to get sympathy from the bystanders.

But Mrs Collins, for one, wasn't impressed. She didn't even appear to have heard what he said. She was busy leaning over to look at the footprint on Bill Simpson's frock.

'This is shocking, Rohan,' she said. 'Shocking! To leave a footprint as clear as this on the frock, you must have lashed out really hard with your foot.'

'I was punched first!'

But Rohan's wailing did him no good. A look of scorn came over Mrs Collin's face. Though she said nothing out loud, you could almost hear her thinking: *How could a little thump on the shoulder from someone in a pretty pink frock excuse a great big kick from someone wearing heavy Doc Marten boots?*

So, thought Bill Simpson quietly to himself.

There can be *one* advantage to wearing a frock.

It didn't last for long, though. She punished them both. She put them at neighbouring desks, and made them write *Fighting is stupid and fighting is ugly* in their best handwriting over and over again, till the bell rang.

They sat with exactly the same sour look on their faces. Both were still furious at the unfairness of it all. To everyone else, they looked for all the world like a pair of scowling and bad-tempered twins.

And every now and again, someone would tiptoe past and whisper in Rohan's ear:

'You look so *angry*.'

But in Bill's they whispered:

'You look so *upset*.'

· 6 ·

Letting Paul Win

As soon as the bell rang for the end of the lunch break, the sun began to shine again. It sailed out from silvery edges of cloud, and blazed over the playground.

The puddles on the tarmac steamed gently, and then disappeared. The damp stains on the nursery wall dried. Sunlight reflected brightly off the rooftops.

Mrs Collins stared out of the window, shaking her head in quiet disbelief. Then she turned to the class.

'Pack up your work,' she said. 'I don't care if lunch break is over. We're going outside before it starts raining all over again.'

The class was astonished. It wasn't often Mrs Collins ignored the timetable on the back of the door. It was hard enough to get her to let them take time off to make decorations at Christmas, or paint the back-cloth if they did a little play. Now here she was offering an hour or so in the sunshine without being asked.

Nobody argued. They slid their books into neat piles, and put their pens and pencils and rubbers away.

'Races!' said Mrs Collins. 'We'll have a few races. We haven't had races for *such* a long time.'

They spilled down the steps out into the playground, and Mrs Collins led them quietly round to the back of the nursery where there was grass. Races were pleasanter on grass, and this patch was not even overlooked by classes still imprisoned in front of their work books.

Out here they could have a really good time.

The races came in every size and description, one after another, as fast as Mrs Collins could think them up. The light haired raced against the dark haired. The straight haired raced against the curly haired.

'Those in frocks against those in trousers!' roared Mrs Collins.

She looked round. Only Bill had a frock on.

'Forget it!' called Mrs Collins. 'That race is cancelled. Think of something else!'

Someone did. Those wearing red raced against those wearing no red at all. Those who liked cats better than dogs raced against those who preferred dogs to cats. The first five in the class (in alphabetical order) raced against the next five, and so on and so on.

The first few times he ran, Bill slowed himself up, trying to keep down the flapping sides of his dress. Then he stopped bothering. If he were in shorts, he wouldn't mind, he decided. So why risk losing a good race just because he was haunted by a silly pink frock. He might be right back to normal tomorrow – but you could just bet there wouldn't be races again!

Soon everyone, not just Bill, felt much better. Their bodies unstiffened, their heads felt clearer, their spirits rose. Even Paul, who had a serious illness when he was a baby and could hardly run, scampered about, enjoying coming in last in the races.

Mrs Collins had cheered up enormously, too.

'Those who have real tin dustbins against those whose families put rubbish out in large, plastic bags!'

Everyone has rubbish. So everyone stood in line.

'There's far too many again,' said Mrs Collins. 'We shall have to have heats.'

As usual she divided them in fives, with one left over. This time it was Paul, so she sent him off in a heat of his own. He pranced along in his curious, loping fashion, and threw himself merrily over the finishing line.

'I'm in the finals now! I won my heat!'

Mrs Collins pushed the hair back from her face. She was hot.

'Small break before this final,' she called. 'All of you stay here quietly while I slip inside for a moment. *Whispering only!*'

And she hurried off to fetch a quick drink.

Bill tucked the pink frock in tightly around his legs and lay back. The grass felt tickly under his arms and his neck. Above, the fat clouds sailed over an enormous sky. The cool breeze fanned his face. He felt perfectly happy.

He heard Astrid whispering in his ear:

'You're in this final, aren't you? You won your heat. So did I. So did Talilah and Kirsty.'

74

'And Paul,' Bill reminded Astrid. 'He won his heat, too.'

He narrowed his eyes against the sunlight to make them water and form rainbows between his eyelashes.

'Kirsty will win,' said Astrid. 'She's the best runner in the whole class. And I only won my heat because Nicky tripped.'

'Races aren't nearly so much fun,' said

Talilah, 'when you know exactly who's going to win.'

'It must be much worse,' whispered Kirsty, 'if you're someone like Paul, and know you're going to lose.'

'Paul can't have won a race in his whole life!'

Bill blinked the rainbows away. Now he was seeing shapes in clouds – a pig, a jug, a serpent with three heads, a wigwam.

Beside him, the girls were in one of their huddles, still whispering away.

'What if Paul *did* win, though?'

'He'd be so *thrilled*.'

'Wouldn't his Mum be pleased? She's so nice. She sees me over Blackheath Road every morning.'

'She'd think we'd fixed it so her Paul won, though. *And* so would Paul.'

'Not if we were clever.'

'Not if we thought it out first, and made it look *good*.'

Bill barely listened. He was distracted by the clouds still. He watched his three-headed serpent float over the wide sky overhead, and turn, slowly, slowly, into a giant wheelbarrow.

The whispering at his side went on and on. Then:

'Right,' Kirsty said. 'That's *settled*.'

She turned to Bill.

'Now don't *forget*,' she whispered sternly. 'Just as you're reaching the line, you get a really bad attack of stitch. You can't go on. You let Paul go past you. You let Paul win, is that understood?'

Bill took a last look at his cloud wheelbarrow. One of its handles was just floating away.

'Right-ho,' he agreed. It wasn't exactly his idea of a really good race – letting Paul win. But that was girls for you, wasn't it? Put them in a group and *order* them to whisper, and they'd be bound to come up with something like this.

And what did it matter on such a lovely afternoon? If it would make Paul happy, let him win the race.

'*On your marks!*'

Mrs Collins strode round the corner. They jumped to their feet. Astrid looked horrified.

'The back of your dress is *covered* with grass stains!' she said to Bill. '*And* they're the sort that never come out!'

Bill shrugged, and made for the starting line. Paul was already there, hopping about with excitement. Astrid, Talilah and Kirsty took their places.

'*Get set!*'

Kirsty turned to Bill.

'Bad luck, then,' she whispered, and grinned.

Bill winked back.

'*Go!*'

Talilah, Kirsty and Bill set off running. Paul shot away from the line in one of his extraordinary leaps. And as soon as he was a few feet ahead of Astrid, she fell tidily sideways and rolled on the ground, clutching her foot.

'Oh, my ankle!' she groaned – but softly, so that Paul would not overhear her, and turn back to help. 'My ankle's gone all wobbly. I can't run at all.'

Then, cheerfully, she picked herself up and, limping heavily on the wrong foot, returned to the others waiting around the line.

'Bad luck!'

'Never mind, Astrid!'

Up at the front of the race, Kirsty and Talilah seemed to be battling it out for first place. Now Kirsty had the edge, now Talilah. Then Kirsty was in front again. But just as she might have pulled ahead of Talilah, the two girls' bodies seemed to become entangled: ankles wrapped round ankles, legs wrapped round legs.

Together they fell, rolling over and over on the grass, giggling loudly.

As Bill ran up, they managed somehow to roll in his way and bring him to a standstill. Twice he tried to get round them, but they rolled the way he was going. Paul was catching up behind, so finally Bill just jumped over their wildly flailing arms and legs. As he did so, he saw Kirsty wink.

Of course! He'd almost forgotten! Let Paul win!

And now there were only himself and Paul left in the race. And so he would have to fall back and let him pull ahead very soon. The winning line was not all that far away. He was already halfway round the circuit.

Right then.

Bill tried to slow his pace. He couldn't do it. It was remarkable, but though he could pound along like a well-oiled machine, and leap over tufts of rough grass without thinking, and even do a fancy sideways hop when he saw something glinting like broken glass beneath his foot, he couldn't slow down. He just couldn't do it.

He couldn't let Paul win.

And it wasn't as if who won the race was important. He knew that. A race might start with those who walked to school running against those who came on a bus or by car, but by the time someone had won, no one could even remember what the race was about.

So it wasn't important.

But still he couldn't slow up and let Paul win. It would look quite ridiculous, he thought. Everyone would guess, and Paul would be really embarrassed.

And then he remembered that he wasn't *supposed* to slow down. The girls had sat in their huddle and worked all this out before the race began. They'd *known* he wouldn't be able to slow down. They'd thought it all out – weren't girls *amazing*?

He was supposed to pretend to have a stitch.

Right, then.

But he couldn't do that, either! And time was running out so fast. He'd almost completed the circuit. There was the finishing line, looming up only a few metres ahead. And there was the whole class, watching.

And he could not stop and double over, grimacing and clutching his stomach as though in the grip of a fierce spasm of pain, pretending he had a stitch.

It wasn't that he couldn't act. It wasn't that he would feel embarrassed about it. It was simply that he could not bring himself to do it. There was the finishing line, and here was he, and there was Paul a really long way behind him now. He wanted to reach the line first, that was all. He didn't want to let Paul win.

He wanted to win *himself*.

Ten metres to go. Now or never. The girls would *kill* him if he let them down.

Five metres. Now or never. Surely even the girls, if they had come this far, would find it difficult to stop and lose.

Three metres. Now or never.

One metre. Now.

There! Over the line!

(Never).

A smile of triumph spread across his face. He'd won. He'd *won!*

He shut his eyes, the better to appreciate the sound of hands clapping, and the cheers.

Then, opening them, he met a cold,

hostile glare from Astrid. And one from Kirsty. And one from Talilah.

There was everybody else, cheering and applauding madly. And there were three pairs of witch eyes, glowering at him balefully.

He'd let them down horribly. It was almost as if he'd cheated to win the race. And since all three had dropped out one after another, expecting that he would as well, he had in a way won it unfairly. If everyone had run properly, Kirsty would almost certainly have won.

The victorious smile on Bill's face faded. He felt small and selfish and ungenerous. He felt ashamed.

But while Bill was standing, picking miserably at the embroidered roses on his pink frock, feeling quite rotten and wishing that everybody would stop cheering, Paul was still bravely pressing round the last bit of the circuit in his funny loping way. And he looked happy enough. He had a huge smile on his face. In fact, he looked positively radiant.

He threw himself across the finishing line, and lay like a tortoise on its back, beaming up at the sky.

'Second!' he yelled in triumph. 'I came second! *Second!*'

Everyone was cheering and clapping for Paul now.

Bill joined in, louder than anybody else.

'Hurray for Paul!' he yelled. 'Second!'

And he reached down to help Paul up.

Paul was a bit unsteady on his feet after the run. Whether it was excitement or exhaustion, Bill didn't know. But Mrs Collins took one brief look at Paul's thin, trembling legs, and said:

'That's it! That was the very last race! Well done, everybody!'

Happily they all trooped back towards the classroom. Astrid and Talilah came up on either side of Paul just in time to hear him confessing excitedly:

'I've never come second in a race before. *Never!*'

Kirsty came up behind Bill, and drew him quietly to one side.

'You just weren't listening, were you?' she scolded. 'Lying there on your back staring at clouds, away with the fairies. You were supposed to pretend to get a stitch!'

'I'm sorry,' said Bill.

'It doesn't matter,' Kirsty said. 'In fact it was probably all for the best. If he'd come first, Paul might have guessed.'

She turned to face him.

'It's just – ' Now, tipping her head to one

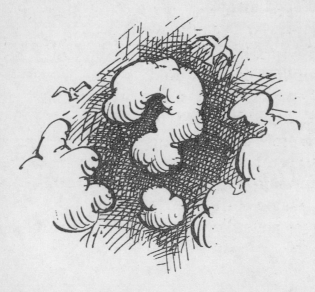

side, she looked him very closely in the eye.
'It's just –'

'*What?*'

Kirsty shook her head, sighing.

'It's just that somehow you seem *different* today. I can't think what it is about you that's odd. But you're not *you*.'

She turned to go.

Bill reached out to try to stop her.

'But who am I?' he asked her desperately. 'Who *am* I?'

But Kirsty, the fastest runner in the class, had sped away.

· 7 ·

Happy Ending

Maybe the day had been more tiring than he realised. Maybe the school work was harder than usual. Bill wasn't sure. All he knew was, he'd had enough. He wanted to go home. It had been the most horrible of days, and he'd be glad to have it over.

The clock hands seemed to crawl. Each

time he looked up, they had scarcely moved. The afternoon seemed endless – *endless*.

And then, at last, the bell rang. And after the usual shouting and clattering and slamming of desk lids, everyone made for the door.

As Bill went past her, Mrs Collins stretched out a hand to hold him back for just a moment.

'You're still not looking quite right to me,' she said. 'I can't work out what it is. But let's hope that you're your old self tomorrow!'

'Yes,' Bill agreed with her fervently. 'Let's hope!'

He had his doubts, though. And it was a dispirited Bill Simpson who trailed down the school drive, dragging his feet. At the gates, Paul was jumping up and down beside his baby sister's push-chair, excitedly telling his mother about the race. They smiled and waved, but Bill pretended not to see.

He was, it has to be admitted, in the worst

mood. He felt angry and bitter and resentful. And he was so sick of the silly pink frock that he would have liked the ground to open and swallow him.

But no such luck. In fact, worse was to come, it seemed. For there at the corner, nesting on one of the dustbins, was Mean Malcolm, waiting for his gang.

Mean Malcolm saw him coming, and whistled.

Bill looked a sight. He knew it. The frock was a rumpled mess, with grubby fingerprints all round the hem, a huge, brown football-shaped smudge on the front, paint smears down the folds, rips in each side where he had hunted in vain for pockets, a great criss-cross footprint where Rohan kicked him, and grass stains down the back – the sort of grass stains that *never* come out.

The frock was a disaster.

And that is probably why, when Mean Malcolm whistled at Bill Simpson again, he took it so very badly.

He stopped and glowered at Mean Malcolm.

'Whistling at *me?*'

Mean Malcolm looked astonished to find this pink apparition glaring at him with such menace. He shifted uneasily on the lid of his dustbin.

'*Because,*' continued Bill savagely, 'I am not a *dog!* I am – '

He hesitated a moment, not knowing quite how to finish; then yelled triumphantly:

'I am a *person!*'

And charging at Mean Malcolm with all the pent-up fury of the most horrible and frustrating day in his life, he flung him backwards off the dustbin lid, into a pile of spilled rubbish.

'There!' he yelled. 'That will teach you! Whistle at dogs in future – not at people!'

And he strode off towards home, a little more cheerful, leaving Mean Malcolm desperately trying to brush the carrot peelings and tea leaves off his purple

studded jacket before his gang came round
the corner and saw him.

When Bill Simpson walked in the front
door of his house, his mother was just
coming in through the back door.

They met in the hall.

Mrs Simpson stopped in her tracks. She
stared at Bill in absolute horror.

'Look at you!' she declared. '*Look* at you! What a mess! Fingerprints! Smudges! Paint smears! Rips! Footprints! Turn around!'

Obediently, Bill spun round. He heard his mother gasp.

'Grass stains!' she shrieked. 'The kind that *never* come out!'

Bill shrugged. It wasn't his fault, after all. He never *asked* to wear the silly frock.

Bill's mother sighed.

'You'd better take it off at once,' she said, unzipping the back and starting to undo the fiddly shell buttons. 'This is the last time I ever send *you* to school in a frock!'

She peeled the offending dress up over his head, and gave him a little push towards the stairs.

Bill needed no prompting. He ran up to his bedroom and pulled on a pair of jeans and a shirt.

Then he took the tiniest, sideways peep in his mirror.

And then another, slightly longer, peep.

And then a good, long stare.

He was a boy! Some people might have said that he could have done with a bit of a haircut . . . But he was definitely a boy.

Never in his whole life had Bill felt such relief.

Bella the cat came up and rubbed her soft, furry body around his ankles in the usual way. She didn't seem to notice any difference.

Bill picked her up and buried his face in her fur.

'It's all right,' he whispered to her delightedly. 'It's over. It's *over*. It doesn't matter if it was a dream, or not. *Whatever it was*, it's all over.'

She purred contentedly in his arms. He held her tight.

'And Mum says,' he repeated firmly to himself and Bella. 'That is the last time I *ever* go to school in a frock!'

And it was.